A Question of Time

A Question of Time
by Dina Anastasio

illustrated by Dale Payson

Random House/New York

For Kristy and Trey, with love
and for Ellen Rudin, with thanks

1

Syd opened her eyes and glanced out the window. It was a perfect day for the zoo. She turned over and looked at the clock. Nine. She threw back the covers and jumped out of bed. There was a knock on the door.

"Come in," she said.

Her mother came in and sat on the bed. "What're you up to?" she asked.

Syd pulled a pair of jeans out of the closet. "Gotta hurry. I'm supposed to meet Jill in Central Park in an hour."

Mrs. Stowe patted the bed. "Sit down, Syd," she said. "I'd like to talk to you."

"Can't."

"It's important."

Syd sat beside her mother and waited.

"Well," Mrs. Stowe said, "I guess there's only one way to say it." She cleared her throat and smiled. "We're moving out of New York."

Syd stared, hoping that she had misunderstood.

"Daddy and I have been thinking about it for a long time, and we've decided to do it."

Syd felt as if someone had knocked the wind out of her. "But why?" she cried.

"I guess we've just had it with the city. Daddy wants to be his own boss, and there's a nice hardware store there that he can buy."

"There's a nice hardware store where?"

"In a small town in Minnesota. And there's a small college that has a job for me, so it's perfect.

"But I don't want to leave New York!" Syd said desperately.

"I know, Syd. And I'm sorry, really I am. But you'll like Parkersburg too, you'll see."

Syd sat up straight and stared at her mother. "Parkersburg? Isn't that where Jake's from?"

"That's right."

"Didn't he say he hated it there? Isn't that why he left?"

"I guess he did. But Jake's a city person. And we've decided that we're not."

"*I'm* a city person!" Syd reminded her.

Mrs. Stowe smiled and stood up. "Maybe, but you've never lived anywhere else. So how do you know?"

"I could stay here with Jake," Syd suggested.

"No, dear," her mother said. "I'm afraid not."

For the first time since school was out, Syd took her time dressing. It was as if the spark had gone out inside of her. She called Jill to tell her she'd be late. Then she went downstairs to her great-grandfather's apartment.

"Did they tell you?" she asked when Jake opened the door.

"I'm afraid so."

"It's an awful town, isn't it?"

Jake smiled and sat on the couch. "I have no idea," he said. "I haven't lived there since I was eighteen, which is, let's see, I'm ninety-five now. . . ."

Syd closed her eyes and subtracted. "Seventy-seven years," she said after a minute.

"That's right. So who knows? It must have changed a lot."

Syd flopped down beside him. "I doubt it," she muttered.

"You'll like it, Syd," Jake said. "You'll see."

"You didn't. You hated it."

"I didn't hate it."

"Then why did you leave?"

"Because I wanted to be an actor. And in 1901, if you wanted to be an actor, you headed for New York."

"But you told me you hated it."

Jake shook his head slowly and sighed. "I didn't hate it, Sydell. I just didn't like it very much."

Syd remembered very clearly that Jake had used the word *hate*, but she decided not to pursue it.

"Did you ever go back?" she asked.

"Just once."

"If you hated, uh, didn't like it, then why'd you go back?"

Jake chuckled and said, "That's better. I went back to make up with my family. They hadn't been too happy about my leaving or becoming an actor. But when I got there, I found that they had all died while I was away. I hadn't heard, because no one knew where I was."

Despite herself, Syd was interested. "They all died?"

"Yes," said Jake.

3

Syd put her feet up on the couch and hugged her knees. When he didn't say anything else, she looked at Jake and said, "Well, I'm going to hate it! I just know I am!"

The hardest part would be saying good-bye to Jill. Saying good-bye to a friend is always difficult, but saying good-bye to someone who has been your very best friend for more than five years, ever since the first grade, is a terrible thing. Syd decided not to do it.

"Let's not say good-bye," she told Jill a week before she was to leave.

"Why not?" Jill asked.

"Let's just wave or something. Saying good-bye seems, I don't know, too final."

Jill came over the night before Syd left. They talked about the past and what the future might bring. And when it was time for Jill to go home, Syd walked her to the elevator. As the doors began to close, they raised their hands and waved. But it didn't fool either of them. They both knew it meant good-bye.

2

A week later, at six o'clock in the morning, Syd opened her eyes and stared at the stark white walls of her new room. It's like waking up in an igloo, she thought. A great flood of light was shining through the huge window directly into her eyes. She slid back down in her sleeping bag and covered her head until she heard her mother moving around in the kitchen. Then she dressed quickly and went downstairs.

"You're up early again," Mrs. Stowe said.

Syd hoisted herself onto the counter and took a doughnut out of the box. "There's too much light in my room here," she said.

"And you don't like that?"

"I like to sleep."

"Did you ever think of curtains?"

Syd hadn't thought of curtains, but she wasn't going to say so. "It'll still be light."

"Of course it won't," her mother told her. "And you know it won't. You're just looking for something to be wrong."

6

Mr. Stowe came into the kitchen and took a doughnut out of the box. "What's going on?" he asked his daughter.

"Syd's room seems to be too light," Mrs. Stowe said.

Mr. Stowe laughed. "I wish that's all we had to worry about. The moving van's coming today, and we've got a million things to do."

Syd moped around the house until the van came. But when she saw her things again, she forgot for a little while that she was a misplaced person. She unpacked her doll collection and placed each doll carefully in the case that she had made the year before. There were dolls that her grandparents had brought back from trips to Germany and Italy, and dolls that her uncle, who was in the army, had brought her from Vietnam, and Japan, and Korea. There were dolls that were very old, and dolls that she had made herself, from things like clothespins and dried apples.

Syd spent most of the next week arranging her room and helping her parents settle into the house and the hardware store. When her room was perfect, her mother bought some curtains and hung them, and the next morning Syd slept until ten.

In her first letter to Jill, she did not mention Parkersburg at all. She wrote only about New York.

. . . And do you remember riding down Fifth Avenue
on our skateboards and imitating the dummies in the
store windows? And asking the baby animals in the
children's zoo if they ever got tired of being petted
by little kids? And the time we named the lion statues
in front of the library Oscar and Matilda?

"Sydell," her mother said one day, "why don't you get out of the house? At least come shopping with me?"

7

But Syd just didn't care about the town or the people in it. The only place that she would go to was her father's store.

"I'll go down to the store again," she told her mother.

On the way home she passed a fence covered with roses. They had a wonderful smell, and for a moment Syd let herself enjoy the trees and the flowers and the squirrels of Parkersburg. This is something that New York doesn't have, she thought. But then she remembered riding her bike through Central Park, and she whispered, "New York has everything."

In two weeks, the house and the store were ready, and there was nothing left to do. Syd's father didn't need her help anymore, and her mother was ready to start her new job. And Syd was left all alone.

3

"You've got to get out of this house," Mrs. Stowe told her daughter a few days later. "You just can't sit here like this forever."

Syd was sitting at the kitchen table, eating a piece of toast and reading her daily letter from Jill. "Why not?" she mumbled, without looking up.

"Because this isn't like you at all."

Syd folded the letter and put it into her pocket. "I just don't fit here," she said. "And I know nobody's going to like me. I'm different, that's all."

Mrs. Stowe smiled. "Come on, Syd," she said. "The kids'll probably like you very much, just because you *are* different. You can offer them something new."

"Ha! Kids aren't like grown-ups. They hate new things."

Mrs. Stowe stood up and started to clear the table. "Well, school starts in a few weeks, and you'll meet plenty of people then."

"I'm not sure I even want to meet them."

Syd went outside. Down the block, some children were playing jump rope in the middle of the street. While two of them turned the ends, the others took turns jumping in and out of the rope without missing a beat. Syd had never played that kind of jump rope before.

She stepped on her skateboard and rode toward them. The children stopped playing and watched as she went by.

"She's good," Syd heard one of them say. She lowered her head and concentrated on the sidewalk in front of her, trying hard to act as if she hadn't heard.

In the middle of the next block, she saw a small toy store and she stopped to look at some tiny finger puppets in the window. Then she picked up her skateboard and opened the door. The bell above the door tinkled as she went in.

"May I help you?" a voice greeted her. The voice belonged to a pleasant-looking woman who was standing behind a cash register.

"I don't know," Syd said. "I guess I'm just looking."

"Anything special?"

"Well, dolls maybe. It's just something to do."

The woman laughed gently. "I see," she said. "One of those long summers?"

The bell tinkled again and a very old man came in. He put a box on the counter. "Wait till you see what I have today, Mrs. Diaz," he said as he opened the box.

As Syd watched, the man took out a doll and stood it on the counter. Syd and Mrs. Diaz looked at it for a long time.

"Why it's the best yet," Mrs. Diaz said at last.

The doll was about a foot tall. It was dressed in blue pants

and a blue shirt, and it looked exactly like a real man, right down to the tiniest fingernail. He looked young, maybe a teen-ager, and he was tall and thin, with dark hair. His right arm and his face were raised, as if he were reaching and looking at something above him.

The woman told Syd: "Mr. Stowe makes dolls that look like the people who used to live in this town."

"Mr. Stowe?"

"That's right," Mrs. Diaz said.

"But that's my name too."

Mr. Stowe smiled at Syd. "Is it?" he said. Then he pointed to a shelf behind her. "Do you see those dolls? I made them so that those people won't be forgotten."

There were three dolls on the shelf, and each was as real looking as the one on the counter. There was a blond man, a girl of about eleven, the same age as Syd, and an old-man doll. The blond man was dressed in blue overalls and a plaid shirt, and he was a bit overweight. On his arm there was a basket of bread. The old-man doll had white hair, and he was dressed in brown baggy pants, a white shirt with a high collar, and suspenders. But Syd couldn't see his face. He was seated on a small brown chair, leaning forward, and in one hand he held a tiny paintbrush.

Syd took the third doll down from the shelf. The girl was wearing a red skirt that came to just below her knees, and a matching red jacket with big puffy sleeves. On her head was a sailor hat with a red ribbon, and she was wearing high pointed shoes. In one hand she held a small suede bag. Syd opened the bag carefully. Inside were three tiny marbles. She was about to replace the doll, when she noticed the look on its small face. It was the saddest face that Syd had ever seen.

"Why is she so unhappy?" she asked the old man.

"She wasn't always."

"What do you mean?"

But Mr. Stowe didn't answer. He just sighed and turned to Mrs. Diaz. "I'm afraid that's the last one," he said. "I won't be making any more."

"Why Mr. Stowe, that's terrible. Your dolls are the best things in the store."

"Well, we'll see," the old man told her. "But right now I've got to be going."

Syd waited until the door had closed behind him. Then she said, "I think he knows who I am."

"Maybe."

"But how?"

"Well, it's a small town. Word travels fast around here."

Syd returned the doll to the shelf. "Tell me some more about Mr. Stowe."

"I'm afraid there isn't much to tell. He brought in the first doll a week ago. He said that he'd be making a few dolls that look just like some people he knew a long time ago. He wanted to sell them as a set. I liked them so much that I agreed. Even now I don't want to sell them."

"I can see why," Syd said. "They sure are interesting."

Syd told Mrs. Diaz about her doll collection. "But I don't have any as nice as these."

Mrs. Diaz nodded. "I don't think anyone does."

14

4

That night at dinner, Syd told her parents about the dolls. "The old-man doll is interesting," she said, "because you can't tell what he's doing."

"Trying to read something?" her father said.

"But why the paintbrush?" Syd asked.

Her father laughed. "Maybe he's painting by numbers."

"The other doll's interesting too," Syd said. "You know, the man who's looking up. I think he might be a basketball player."

"Could be," her father agreed.

"I forgot the most important thing," Syd said. "The old man who makes the dolls—well, guess what his name is."

"What?" her father asked.

"Mr. Stowe."

"And I'll bet you think he's a long lost relative of ours."

"Well, couldn't he be?"

"Anything's possible. But I doubt it."

"But I think he knew *my* name was Stowe."

15

"In a small town," her mother told her, "people know things like that."

"That's what the woman in the store said."

"And she's right," Mrs. Stowe said.

"Well, I'm going to ask him anyway," Syd told them. "Wouldn't it be fun if he knew Jake?"

"It sure would," her father said. He started to clear the table and Mrs. Stowe got up to help him. Syd put away the salt and pepper. From the kitchen she heard her father say, "She seems to be getting back to normal."

"Sort of," her mother said.

The next day, Syd was at the toy store when it opened.

"You're up bright and early," Mrs. Diaz said.

"I've been thinking about those dolls."

She went over to the shelf and took down the old-man doll. She turned it around and around, trying to figure out what he was doing. But his head was covering whatever was in his lap, and she couldn't tell.

"You know," she told Mrs. Diaz, "last night I was lying in bed, trying to picture the dolls as real people. Like sad-eyed girl."

"Sad-eyed girl?"

"Well, okay," Syd laughed. "I know it sounds weird, but I've named them. There's sad-eyed girl, the basketball player, the bread man, and this one—the old man. Anyway," Syd continued, "I can imagine what all the others were like. But this old man is driving me nuts."

Syd put the doll on the counter and tried to move the head so that she could see the face. But it was no use. It wouldn't budge. Next she touched the tiny paintbrush, but it held no clues. Then she touched the other arm, and it moved. Syd moved the arm a little more, and then a little more, until she found what it was that the old man was painting. He was painting the hands on a tiny toy pocket watch. Syd took a magnifying glass off a shelf and studied the watch very carefully. Both hands, she noticed, were pointing toward the twelve.

She put the doll back on the self. "He's painting a watch," she told Mrs. Diaz. "It says twelve o'clock."

"I wonder what that means. Do you think he fixed watches?"

"Maybe." Syd sighed and leaned on the counter. "What if I ask Mr. Stowe?"

"Good idea," Mrs. Diaz said.

"I wish I knew where to find him," Syd said. "If he comes back while I'm not here, don't forget to ask him."

Mrs. Diaz smiled. "I won't forget."

"And ask him if we're related."

"I will."

5

The next morning Syd went to the library and looked in the card file under "Parkersburg." There were three books, but only one seemed as if it might be what she was looking for. The book was called *This Is Parkersburg,* and it was published in 1900.

Syd sat down with it at a table. It was a small book, with only fifty pages, and at least half of the pages were photographs. She thumbed through it quickly.

"I'd like to check this out," she told the librarian.

The woman picked up the book and opened the front cover. "This is a seven-day book, you know," she said.

"What's a seven-day book?"

"It means you can keep it for only seven days."

"Oh, that's okay. But why only seven days?" Syd was used to one-month books.

"It's special. The man who wrote it was a printer, and he made only one copy. He gave it to the library as a gift, along with three or four other books that he had printed. We've had it a

long, long time, and so far everybody's been very careful with it."

"I'll be careful," Syd promised.

"I'm sure you will," the librarian said. Then she made out a temporary card in Syd's name and checked out the book.

On the way home, Syd stopped to sniff the roses on the fence. They smelled so good. Come to think of it, although Central Park had trees and squirrels, she had never seen any roses there.

At home, she went straight to her room and began to read.

By eight o'clock each morning, the corner of Fourth and Main is alive with the sounds of people selling their wares. Shopkeepers are opening their doors. Bakers are forming their first loaves of the day. Children are on their way to school.

Syd looked at the picture on the first page. Three women, dressed in long dresses, were standing in a group on a street corner. Small shops lined one side of the unpaved street. On the other side there was a large white church. And next to it, Syd noticed with a grin, was a pool hall.

Syd opened the top drawer of her desk and took out a magnifying glass. That was much better. She moved the glass slowly over the picture. There. Directly in the middle was the basketball player. He was wearing the same pants and shirt, and he seemed to be walking very quickly.

Syd turned the page to the next picture. The caption described Fourth and Main at noon. The picture showed a street crowded with people, horse-drawn buggies and bicycles. Under the magnifying glass, she found the bread man standing in front of a small bakery.

Syd read the whole book carefully. By the time she had

21

reached the last page, she knew a lot about the town. But she still hadn't found the old man with the paintbrush.

She turned back to the picture of Fourth and Main at noon and studied the people and the shops once again. This time she saw him immediately. He was seated behind the window of a shop three doors down from the bakery.

The sign in the window read: Joseph's Toy Shop.

"So that's what he does," Syd said to herself. "He's not a watch repairman. He's a toy maker."

Outside the toy shop, near the door, a girl of about Syd's age was playing marbles. And although her head was bent, she looked a great deal like the sad-eyed doll in Mrs. Diaz's toy store.

Syd went back to the library.

"You didn't have to bring it back that fast," the librarian said when she saw Syd.

"I wanted to ask you something."

"Okay. Go ahead."

"Well, I was wondering if an old man has taken this book out recently."

The librarian looked at the card in the back of the book. "You're the first person who's taken this book out in years."

"Well then," Syd asked, "have you ever seen an old man around here?" And she described Mr. Stowe carefully.

But the librarian hadn't seen him. Syd handed her the book. Then she asked all of the other people who worked in the library if they had seen Mr. Stowe. But none of them had seen him either.

He must have used this book to make the dolls, Syd thought. No one can remember exactly how a person looks after seventy-eight years.

22

6

The next morning Syd rode her bike to the corner of Fourth and Main. She had been picturing it as it was in 1900, but of course it was quite different. The streets were paved. The small shops had been replaced by bigger stores. The horses and bicycles had made way for cars.

Syd locked her bike and walked up the street. She went into a drugstore with a soda fountain and booths on one side. She sat down at the counter and ordered a large dish of chocolate ice cream.

As she ate, she watched the people walking by the store window. She thought of all the Saturdays in New York when she and Jill had gone to the pizza parlor on the corner and watched the people together.

Syd would have given anything to have Jill here now. Jill would have loved the dolls. And she would have loved looking them up in the book in the library. But most of all, she would have loved trying to figure out how Mr. Stowe had remembered

all of the details so well. But Jill was back in New York, and there was nothing that Syd could do about it.

Two girls came into the drugstore and sat in a booth near the back. Syd watched them out of the corner of her eye. Pretty soon she noticed that the girls were peeking at her in the same way, and it made her smile. The girls were leaning back against the wall with their legs resting on the seats in front of them, as if they owned the booth, and Syd wondered if she would ever feel that way about this place or any other place in Parkersburg.

She put her change into her pocket and went outside. Next door was a hobby shop, and Syd turned to look at the trains in the window.

"Watch it!" a voice called. But it was too late. Syd tripped and fell. She stood up quickly and brushed herself off.

"You ought to be more careful," said a girl below her. "You nearly stepped on my hand."

"Sorry."

The girl looked to be about Syd's age, but she was smaller. She was dressed just like Syd, in jeans and a T-shirt. Her hair was dark, and it looked as if someone had put a bowl on her head and cut around it. She was kneeling right in the middle of the sidewalk. You either had to trip over her or walk around her.

"What are you doing?" Syd asked.

"Playing marbles."

Syd had never played marbles, but she had read a lot about the game in books. Lots of people who lived in the country played marbles. But she had never heard of anyone playing the game right smack in the middle of a busy sidewalk.

"Isn't this an odd place to play?" she asked.

The girl just shrugged and said, "I always play here."

"I thought you had to play marbles in the dirt."

"You usually do. But you can draw a circle, like this one, on the sidewalk."

Syd watched the girl pick up a clear blue glass marble and shoot it at the marbles in the circle. "How can you play alone?" she asked. "I thought you had to shoot the other player's marbles out of the circle."

"You do. But if there's no one to play with, you do the best you can."

Syd watched. Whenever the girl shot a marble, it rolled across the sidewalk and into the street. Then she would jump up and run after it.

After a while Syd couldn't stand it. "Look," she said. "This is silly. Why don't you bring your marbles over to my house and we'll play a game in the dirt."

"I don't know if I can. My grandfather wants me to play right here, so he'll know where to find me."

"When will he be back?"

"He always comes at twelve sharp. Then we go home for lunch."

"Okay," Syd said. "I'll make sure you're back before twelve. It's only eleven now. That's plenty of time."

"Well," the girl said slowly, "I don't know."

"We'll be back by twelve. I promise."

Syd unlocked her bike and waited while the girl gathered up her marbles and put them into a small suede bag. "That's a nice bag," she said. "May I see it?"

"Sure."

"You know," Syd said, "I've seen a bag just like this before."

The girl didn't answer, so Syd shrugged and started to walk her bike. "What's your name?" she asked.

26

"It's Laura," the girl told her.

And then Syd knew that she had seen her face before. She started to say something, but then she looked at Laura again, and she wasn't so sure. The hair was the same, and the suede bag. But this girl was happy, not sad like the doll in the toy store.

7

Laura handed Syd some of her marbles. "The first thing you do is put some marbles in the circle. Then you choose another marble for a shooter. I try to shoot your marbles out with my shooter, and you try to shoot mine out. Whenever you shoot one of my marbles out, you get to keep it."

Syd knelt down on one knee and held her shooter like she had seen Laura hold hers. She aimed for a clear green marble. The shooter rolled slowly into the circle and stopped about six inches from the green marble. "Now what?" she asked.

"It's my turn."

On her first shot, Laura knocked three marbles out of the circle. On her second she knocked out two.

"Hey, you're good," Syd told her.

"I've been playing a long time."

Laura won the first game easily. "Want to play again?" she asked.

Syd stood up and walked over to the big oak tree. She sat

28

down on the swing and looked at Laura carefully. "Let's talk."

Laura stretched out on the grass. "Okay. What'll we talk about?"

"Let's talk about you."

Laura laughed. "I'm pretty boring."

"There's something that's been driving me crazy," Syd told her. "I've got to ask you about it."

"All right."

"Well, there's a toy store near here that sells dolls. An old man named Mr. Stowe makes them. And one of the dolls looks just like you."

Laura turned over and put her head in her arms. She didn't say anything.

"It's weird," Syd went on. "She has the same coloring, and the same haircut. The only thing that's different is her expression. You aren't as sad."

"Maybe this Mr. Stowe saw me and made a doll that looks just like me."

"And she's holding a bag of marbles."

"Well, maybe he saw me playing marbles."

Syd pushed off and began to pump. The swing went higher and higher. "That could be," she called when she was swinging above Laura's head. "But the dolls are supposed to look like people who lived about eighty years ago."

Laura stood up and brushed herself off. "I've got to get back."

"I'll walk downtown with you." The swing slowed to a stop and Syd jumped off.

They started walking back toward town. Syd noticed that the kids down the block were playing jump rope again.

29

"That's another game that I don't know," she told Laura.

"Me either." Laura stopped to watch.

"I thought you were in a hurry."

"Just a minute."

A boy and a girl were turning the ends of the rope. Five other people were standing in line, waiting their turn to jump in. Every time the rope turned, someone jumped in and then out. One beat, one jump.

"Dumb game," Syd whispered.

"No it's not. But it looks hard. I don't think I could do it."

"I could," Syd assured her.

While they played, the other children studied Syd and Laura. One, the girl who was turning the rope, smiled at them. "Do you want to play?" she asked.

"No thanks," Syd said.

"We don't know how," Laura added.

The girl smiled again. "We'll show you."

"Maybe some other time," Syd told her.

They walked on toward town.

"Didn't you think it looked like fun?" Laura asked.

"I guess."

"Hard though."

"I don't know. It's just that, well, we never did stuff like that in New York."

"What did you do in New York?"

"I had this friend, Jill," Syd said slowly, "and we did all kinds of things together."

"And Parkersburg's different?"

"A lot. First of all, there's only one movie theater, and I saw the movie that's playing there over a year ago. And except for that, there's nothing to do."

"You can always learn to play jump rope."

"How come you never did?"

"I don't know. But I wish I had."

"Can you come over again tomorrow?" Syd asked when they reached the hobby shop.

"It depends on my grandfather."

"Well, I'll come down in the morning and see if you're here."

"All right," Laura said. She sat down on the sidewalk and put her marbles in the middle of the chalk circle.

Syd walked up the sidewalk, kicking a small stone. After half a block, she went back.

"There's something I forgot to tell you," she said. "I found a book in the library the other day. It was about Parkersburg in 1900, and there was a picture of a girl playing marbles in the dirt. You know, she looked an awful lot like you."

Laura stopped playing. "I didn't know there was a book," she said, so softly that Syd could barely hear her.

"What?" Syd asked.

"Do you still have the book?"

"No."

"Well, maybe tomorrow we can go to the library, and you can show it to me."

"Oh, good," Syd said. "And then we can go to the toy store and see the doll."

"Great." Laura picked up a marble and began to play. Syd watched for a few minutes. Then she turned and walked home.

8

"I see you've found someone to play with," Mrs. Stowe said at lunch.

"I guess so. But she's kind of weird."

"What do you mean?"

Syd took a bite of a peanut butter sandwich and thought for a minute. "Well, it's not really that *she's* weird. It's more like there's something weird *about* her. Have you ever heard of anyone sitting in the middle of the sidewalk all day?"

"How'd you meet her?"

"I tripped over her."

Mrs. Stowe laughed out loud. "Well, at least you've found somebody." She stood up. "If I don't get over to school, I'll miss my two o'clock meeting. Do the dishes now and stay out of trouble."

When the kitchen was clean, Syd went upstairs and lay down on her bed. She stared at the ceiling for a long time. All of a sudden she realized that she hadn't written to Jill in four days. She had been so busy with the dolls. She sat down at her desk.

Dear Jill,

I can't believe that I haven't written for so long. It's not that I've forgotten you or anything. I just got interested in something. I'll tell you in a minute.

First of all, I've finally been downtown, so I can tell you a little about Parkersburg. Compared to New York, it's tiny. It has two main streets, one library (minus Oscar and Matilda), and a lot of small, but okay, stores.

The kids I've met seem nice, but there's just something about them. I don't know what it is. They just aren't like us. They play jump rope, which is a dumb game. I keep hoping I'll meet someone like you, someone who'll like the same shows on TV, and who'll go to the movies with me.

But, and this is a big but, I have met one friend. She's weird, but maybe that's why she's easy to talk to. Anyway, Laura isn't anywhere *near* as good a friend as you are. Have you met anyone who's a better friend than I am? I hope not!!

Here is the thing I wanted to tell you. . . .

Syd went on to tell Jill about Laura, the dolls in the toy shop, and the book in the library.

Do you think I'm imagining this whole thing? Maybe I am. Maybe they don't look that much alike. I guess I'll know tomorrow when I see Laura and the doll and the book together.

I'll write again when I've got this all figured out. Boy, do I ever wish you were here!!

Love,
Syd

P.S. Could you come out here and visit me over
Christmas vacation? Ask your mom.

Syd went downstairs and got on her skateboard. She rode
down to the corner and dropped the letter into the mailbox.

On the way back, she passed one of the girls who had been
playing jump rope that morning. The girl stopped and watched
as Syd showed off on her skateboard a little bit. First she did a
quick 360, and followed it with a nose wheelie. But when she
tried to jump a curb, she wiped out and landed on the street. For
a minute she was afraid to look up, in case the girl was laughing
at her. But the girl wasn't laughing at all.

She held the skateboard out to Syd. "Are you all right?"

"I'm okay."

"Those tricks sure are neat. Could you teach me some of
them sometime?"

"Sure," Syd said, as she retrieved her skateboard. "How
about now?"

"I can't. I've got to get over to the school, and I'm late already. Say, maybe you'd like to come?"

"What do you do there?"

"We play baseball and kickball, and stuff like that. It's fun.
Why don't you come?"

Syd hesitated. "I guess not. I've got a lot to do today."

"Well, all right."

"Kickball!" Syd said to herself as she watched the girl walk
away. "Only second graders play kickball!"

9

Laura was playing marbles when Syd arrived at nine the next morning.

"Did you stay here all night?" Syd laughed.

Laura smiled. "No, but I've been here for an hour," she said. "My grandfather wanted to get here early. He had some packing to do."

"Are you ready to go to the library?"

Laura stood up and put her marbles into the little suede bag. "Let's go," she said.

They walked in silence for a while.

"What does your grandfather do anyway?" Syd asked finally.

"For the past few weeks he's been working in the hobby shop."

"Oh, that's why he makes you stay in front all day?"

"It's not so bad. I kind of like being near him. I guess I feel safe."

Syd remembered her first two weeks in Parkersburg, and she said, "I can understand that."

At the library, Syd looked up the book again in the card file. But when she went to find it, it wasn't there.

"That's funny," she told Laura. "Nobody's taken that book out in years. And now that we want it, it's gone."

Syd led Laura to the desk. This time the librarian was a man. "I'm looking for a book," she said, "but it's not there. Can you tell me who took it out?"

"Not easily. It would take a lot of searching."

"It's pretty important."

"Did you leave something in the book?"

Syd looked at Laura. "You might say that," she said to the librarian.

"Well, it'll take a little time. Tell me the name of the book and come back in about half an hour."

They went over to the magazine section to wait.

"Do you know a lot of kids in Parkersburg?" Syd asked.

"Not really."

"How long have you lived here?"

"Not long."

Laura opened a magazine and began to read.

She doesn't want to talk about it, Syd thought. She tried to concentrate on a magazine, but she couldn't stop wondering about Laura. When had she come to Parkersburg and where had she come from? She wanted to ask who her friends were, or if she had any friends. But there was something about Laura, something very private, that kept Syd from saying anything.

"Do you think the kids here will like me?" Syd whispered.

"Sure they will," Laura said, without looking up. "Once they get to know you."

"What do you mean?"

"Nothing."

"Come on. What do you mean?"

"Well," Laura said, "sometimes when someone doesn't join in, people think they're snobs."

"You mean people might think that I think I'm better than they are?"

"Well, I know you don't. But other people might get the wrong idea."

"Maybe I do feel that way a little bit," Syd said slowly. "Do you ever feel that way?"

Laura made a sound that was a combination of a chuckle and a sigh. "Sometimes I used to. But then something happened, and people began to look down on me. It felt terrible."

Syd sat back. Laura was beginning to sound like her mother. Give it a chance. Give them a chance. Join in. You're here to stay, so you might as well make the best of it. Say hello. They'll like you. It was just too hard, too complicated. If she could only close her eyes and go back to New York where she belonged, life would be so much easier.

"You know that girl in the book?" Syd said. "The one who looks like you?"

"Yes."

"Do you think she ever felt like this? You know, out of place?"

"Probably," said Laura.

"When I was reading that book, I was thinking how easy it all seemed back then. I'll bet people didn't feel this way at all."

"My grandfather says that people have always felt the same feelings. The way they dress changes, and the way they talk, and things like that. But not the way they feel."

39

Suddenly Syd thought about Jake. "I have a great-grandfather who's ninety-five," she said, "and he says that when he was little he always felt out of place. He came from here, you know, and he never did feel at home here."

"He came from here?"

"A long time ago. Almost eighty years, I guess."

"What's his name?" Laura asked.

"It's Stowe, the same as mine."

Laura sat up straight and stared at Syd. "When did you say he lived here?"

"About 1900, I guess. Why, have you heard of him or something?"

Laura looked down at her magazine. "No, how could I?"

"I don't know. You just looked so funny for a minute."

"I didn't mean to," was all that Laura said. She kept reading her magazine, and Syd had no choice but to do the same.

When their half hour was up, the girls went back to the desk.

"Remember us?" Syd asked the librarian.

"Sure I do. You're the *This Is Parkersburg* girls."

"Do you know who took it out?"

The librarian reached under the desk and took out a slip of paper. "Joseph Stowe."

Syd looked at the librarian for a long time.

"Is anything wrong?" he asked.

"No, no. That's fine. Thanks a lot."

"That's him, you know," Syd said, when the girls were outside.

"That's who?"

"Mr. Stowe, that's who; the man who makes the dolls. I don't get this at all. I could understand if he had taken the book

41

out *before* he made the dolls. But why would he take it out *after* all the dolls are finished?"

"He might not even be the same Mr. Stowe."

"Then there sure are a lot of Stowes around here lately," Syd said. "But there's a way to find out."

She went back into the library. "I forgot to ask you his address," she told the librarian.

The man went over to a card file behind the desk and looked in it. "The only address I have is Lake Drive," he said when he came back. "But that can't be right."

"Why not?"

"Because Lake Drive's a very short road, and it only has one house on it." The librarian looked down at Syd. "Don't tell me you haven't heard about the house on Lake Drive?"

"I'm new here."

"But that's the first story most people hear when they arrive in town."

"Tell me, tell me," Syd said.

"Well, a long time ago there was a murder out there. No one can remember exactly what it was all about, and everybody in town will tell you a different story. You know how rumors are. Anyway, there was a murder, but they never found a body, so they never arrested anyone. The house has been boarded up for as long as I've lived here."

"Boy, is that something," Syd said. "So how could this Mr. Stowe live out there?"

"Don't ask me."

"When did Mr. Stowe get that card?" Syd asked.

The librarian looked in the file. "He got it yesterday."

"Did he have a card before?"

42

"Not according to our records."

"He's never taken a book out before?"

"That's right. You can't take out a book without a card."

Syd hurried outside to tell Laura.

"You still don't know if Mr. Stowe the doll maker, and this Joseph Stowe of Lake Drive are the same," Laura said.

"They have to be. They're both new in town and they have the very same name. They just have to be."

"Well," Laura said vaguely, "he'll probably bring the book back soon, and I can see it then."

But Syd wasn't so sure.

10

Mrs. Diaz was dusting shelves when Syd and Laura came in. "Well hello," she said. "I've missed you."

"I've found someone to play with."

"Is this your new friend?" she asked, looking at Laura.

"Uh-huh. Her name's Laura. This is Mrs. Diaz."

Laura smiled shyly and said hello. Then she turned away and started to look at the toys.

Mrs. Diaz stared after her. "You know," she whispered to Syd, "there's something . . ."

"Familiar?"

"Yes, something familiar."

"You've seen her before?"

"You too?"

"Me too. And I know where."

Syd led Mrs. Diaz over to the doll shelf. The basketball player was there. The bread man was there. The old man was there. But the girl with the marbles was gone.

"She's missing!"

But Mrs. Diaz didn't answer. She was watching Laura.

"Mrs. Diaz, the sad-eyed doll is missing!"

"The one that looks like your friend?"

Syd smiled. "I was beginning to think I was crazy. Do you really think they look alike?"

"Exactly alike."

"Well, where is she?"

Laura came back. "Where is who?" she asked.

"The doll that I was going to show you. She's not here."

The bell above the door tinkled, and a boy came in. Mrs. Diaz went to help him.

"I hope no one bought her," Syd said to Laura.

They waited while Mrs. Diaz put a yo-yo into a bag and handed it to the boy. Laura took the bread man from the shelf.

"Don't drop the little newspaper," Mrs. Diaz said.

Syd and Laura looked at the doll. A tiny newspaper was sticking out of the bread man's basket. Syd tried to read it, but the print was too small. She took a magnifying glass off a shelf.

"There's nothing written on it except the date October 12, 1901." She put the paper back in the basket. "I don't remember seeing this newspaper before," she said to Mrs. Diaz.

"Mr. Stowe brought it in yesterday when he took the sad-eyed doll. He said he wanted to fix something on her."

Syd looked at Laura, who had moved backward and was leaning against the wall. She was playing with the end of her belt.

"First the book and now the doll," Syd said. "Something is very, very weird. I'm going to look for Mr. Stowe and find out exactly what's going on. Oh," she added, turning to Mrs. Diaz, "did you ask him where he lives and if we're related?"

"I'm afraid I didn't have a chance. But I'll ask him next time. He said he'd bring the doll back in a week or so."

"I don't think he'll ever bring it back."

"Why not?"

Syd looked at Laura. "I have a very strange feeling it has something to do with you."

Laura put her hands in her pockets and moved toward the door. "It's almost twelve," she said softly. "I guess I'd better be getting back."

"Wait a minute. I'll come with you," Syd said. But Laura had already gone outside.

Syd hurried toward the door. "By the way," she said to Mrs. Diaz, "did Mr. Stowe ever mention Lake Drive?"

"No, why would he?"

"Because I think he lives on Lake Drive."

"That's impossible."

"Because of the murder?"

Mrs. Diaz laughed. "You certainly do get around."

"What do you know about the murder?"

"Only that somebody who lived there killed somebody else who lived there a long time ago, and no one has lived there since. I know because I've gone swimming out there all my life. When we were kids, we used to think the house was haunted. And I hear that the kids nowadays think so too."

11

"Well, that's it," the librarian said, as he focused the microfilm machine. "Now all you've got to do is read it."

Syd leaned forward and studied the screen in front of her. The machine looked like a large TV set. But instead of seeing a television program, Syd was reading Parkersburg's weekly newspaper, dated October 12, 1901.

Syd studied the page carefully. She wasn't sure what she was searching for, but whatever it was, she knew it had to be there, somewhere. There was a story about a fire, and several stories about club meetings and bake sales. And then she saw it, far down at the bottom left-hand corner of the page.

Strange Happening on Lake Drive

She pulled her chair closer and read the article.

Something strange happened up on Lake Drive at about midnight last night. Danny and Walter Richardson were swimming in the lake, when they heard loud, angry shouts coming from the big house on the hill.

"We were curious," they said later, "so we snuck up the hill to listen. Peter Stowe and his son, Jacob, were having a terrible fight. We listened for a while, and then we heard Peter Stowe shout: 'If you move, I'll kill you.' Well, he sure sounded like he meant it, so we ran down the hill and rode our bicycles back into town to get the marshall."

Marshall Bowman and the boys rode back to the house in the marshall's buggy. But when they arrived, the house was quiet. Jacob Stowe was nowhere to be seen. When asked what had happened to his son, all that Peter Stowe would say was, "I guess he left."

Syd sat back in her chair. Jacob Stowe, she thought. That's Jake's name.

She got up and walked over to the desk. "Could you help me again?" she asked the librarian.

"I'll be right with you," the man told her.

Syd went back to the machine and read the article again. Then she studied some of the ads on the side of the page. The one nearest the top read: "Cut from $3.39 to $1.59. Sailor suits for boys." The ad below it made Syd giggle. "Rid your child of worms with reliable worm syrup. 20¢ a bottle."

"Okay," the librarian said behind her. "What's up?"

"Can you help me find the next week's paper?"

The librarian showed Syd how to move the film forward and backward, and after a few minutes she found the October 19, 1901 paper. This time the article was at the top of the front page. The headline said:

Was Jacob Stowe Murdered?

Syd leaned forward.

Whatever happened to Jacob Stowe? No one has seen him since the night, a week ago, when Peter Stowe was heard to say that he would kill him. Anyone knowing the where-abouts of Jacob Stowe should get in touch with Marshall Bowman. Jacob is 18 years old, and, until last week, lived in the big house out on Lake Drive with his sister, his father, and his grandfather. Jacob's mother has been dead for nine years.

Syd moved the lever and watched as Parkersburg's weekly news moved by on the screen. For the next few weeks there was no mention of the case. But in one of the November papers, she saw the following headline:

Whatever Happened to Jacob Stowe?

and it was followed by a letter to the editor.

Jacob Stowe is still missing, and many people in Parkers-burg are beginning to think that foul play was involved. It is not uncommon to hear talk of murder on the streets and in the shops of Parkersburg these days. I for one feel that a terrible wrong is being done.

Peter Stowe has had to close his store because of lack of business. His father, Joseph Stowe, has done the same. And his daughter has been forced to leave school. Because of the rumors, all three have taken to hiding in shame in the house on Lake Drive. Is this fair, when we don't have the facts; when we don't even know if someone was really murdered?

I ask your help. Give these people a chance.

Syd scanned the papers for the next few months, but she couldn't find anything else about the case.

"I'm through," she told the librarian.

"Did you find what you were looking for?"

"Boy did I! I've been reading all about that murder up on Lake Drive, and guess who was murdered, or who they think was murdered?"

"Who?"

"A man named Stowe. It was back in 1901—and you were right. They never did find a body."

"You know," the man said, "you'd be perfect on our *Kid's Gazette*."

"What's that?"

"It's a little newspaper that a few kids put out. They report on what's happening around town. You might enjoy it, especially since you're so good at doing research. And since you're new, it might be a good way to meet people."

"Maybe," Syd said. "I don't—well, let me think about it, okay?"

"Sure. Take your time."

12

"You don't think there could be two Jacob Stowes who lived here in 1901, do you?" Syd asked her parents at lunch.

"I doubt it," her mother said. "Why?"

Syd told them what she had read in the papers.

"And you think that after Jake left for New York in 1901," Mrs. Stowe said, "everyone in Parkersburg thought his father had killed him?"

"I don't know. Do you?"

"I think we'd better call Jake tonight," her father said, "and see if we can clear some of this up."

Syd stood up. "There are a lot of things I wish someone would clear up," she said. "Like who is this Mr. Stowe that makes the dolls and lives out on Lake Drive? And why did he put that 1901 newspaper in the doll's basket? And how come he keeps taking my book and my doll just when I'm about to show them to Laura? Which is another thing. How come Laura looks so much like that other girl who lived back in 1901?"

"The doll could be her grandmother," Mrs. Stowe said. "And maybe Laura looks like her."

Syd opened the back door. "Hey," she said. "That could be right. I think I'll go downtown and ask her. By the way, can we go to the lake this weekend? It's supposed to be pretty hot."

Mrs. Stowe laughed. "Sure, why not. If it's warm, we'll go Saturday. I'd like to get a look at that house on Lake Drive myself."

Syd went outside and looked in the mailbox. The top letter was from Jill, and Syd put it into her back pocket. I'll read it later, she thought. Then she rode her bike downtown.

Laura was playing marbles in her usual spot. People wove around her, being careful not to step on her hands. Syd went into the drugstore and ordered a double-dip chocolate cone. She was eating it as she walked up to Laura.

"Hi," she said. "Want a lick?"

Laura looked up and shook her head. For a minute neither girl said anything. Then Syd said, "Do you . . . ?" and Laura said, "How's the . . . ?" and they both laughed.

"You go," Syd said.

"I was only going to ask what you've been doing."

"Well, mostly trying to figure out this doll thing."

"Have you learned to jump rope yet?"

"No. But the man at the library told me about a newspaper that some kids put out. I'm thinking about working on that. Being a newspaper reporter might be kind of exciting."

"You could get to know the town that way, and the people."

"I know. But there's not much to report around here."

"Well, it won't be as interesting as New York."

"Listen," Syd said. "Can I ask you something?"

"Sure."

54

"I don't mean to be nosy or anything. But I told my mother about the doll that looks like you. And she thought it might be your grandmother."

"I don't know," Laura said quickly.

"Do you look like your grandmother?"

Laura picked up a marble and leaned over. But she didn't shoot it. She sat back and looked up at Syd.

"I never knew either of my grandmothers," she said. "So I don't know. But no one's ever told me that I look like them. Look, I can't talk about this anymore. It's not that it's none of your business. It's just that . . ." Her voice trailed off. And then she was silent.

"Would it be okay if I asked your grandfather?"

Laura sighed as if it wouldn't be okay at all. "I guess it'll be all right."

"Hey, maybe you could work on that kids' paper with me."

Laura hesitated, and for a minute a sad look came into her eyes. "I wish . . . yes, I'd like that."

"Then it's a deal. We'll tackle this town together. Parkersburg won't even know what hit it."

Laura smiled. "I've been meaning to ask you something too."

"What?"

"I was wondering what your great-grandfather's first name is."

"Jake. Why?"

"I was just interested, that's all."

"But why?" Syd asked again.

"No reason. What does he do?"

Syd looked at Laura carefully. Questions were beginning to play in the corners of her mind, but she didn't know exactly how to ask them.

"He's not doing much right now," she said. "He used to be an actor."

"Was he any good?"

"Very good."

Laura smiled again and said, "I'm glad." Then she picked up a marble and leaned over.

Syd walked around her and went into the hobby shop to talk with Laura's grandfather. A young man was working behind the counter.

"Can I talk to the old man who works here? He's the grand-father of the girl who plays marbles on the sidewalk all day." Syd pointed to the window. But Laura was no longer there.

"Today's the old man's last day. He just went out the back way, and I don't think he's coming back."

"What does he do here?"

The man showed her a door. "He works in there. We have a line of wooden toys that we make ourselves, and he's been help-ing out for the past few weeks."

"May I look in the room?"

"Sure."

Syd walked over to the door and opened it slowly. At the far end of the room was a long workbench. A variety of tools were laid out neatly on it. There was also a box of paints and several paintbrushes. Two large boxes were on the floor behind the bench. One was filled with pieces of wood, and the other held bits of fabric.

Syd closed the door quietly behind her. "I thought you said he made wooden toys," she said to the man.

"That's right."

"Well, why does he have all those pieces of cloth?"

57

"Oh, that's for his own work. He comes in every morning before we open and does some special work of his own."

"What is he making?"

"Dolls, I think."

"Did you say he's not coming back?"

"That's right. He said he was finished with what he'd set out to do."

Syd walked over to the window and looked out. There was no sign of Laura.

"Is his name Mr. Stowe?" she asked the man.

"That's right."

"And is his first name Joseph?"

"I don't know."

"I've got one more question," Syd said. "Do you know what was here before this store?"

"I'm not sure," the man said. "But once, a long time ago, I found an old sign in the back, and it said: Joseph's Toy Shop."

Syd ran her finger along the window and thought about Laura. A sad, lonely feeling spread through her body as she wondered why Laura hadn't told her that her grandfather had made the dolls. Syd had begun to think of Laura as her friend. And now she realized that she didn't know this girl at all.

Syd went outside. As she was unlocking her bike, she remembered Jill's letter, and she took it out of her pocket and opened it. It was a very short letter, only three or four lines, and it wasn't very interesting. For the first time since she'd left New York, Syd realized that her letters from Parkersburg were more interesting than Jill's.

13

Jake answered the phone on the second ring. Although it was only seven o'clock at night, he sounded tired, and Syd said, "Were you asleep?"

"Sydell?"

"Hi, Jake."

"Well my heavens," Jake said, sounding very happy and much less sleepy, "you can wake me anytime. What a nice surprise. How's Parkersburg?"

Syd told him about how the town had changed since 1900, and about their new house.

"But how about friends?" he asked. "Have you made any friends?"

"Well, there are a lot of kids around here. And they're okay, I guess. And I've met a girl named Laura. But there's nobody like Jill."

"That reminds me, Jill's been over a couple of times. She says you don't write very much anymore."

"I know. I kind of got busy."

"You did?" Jake sounded as if there was a smile in his voice. "That seems like a good sign."

"What do you mean?"

"It sounds as if you're becoming a Parkersburgian."

"I am not!" Syd insisted hotly. "I'm just busy, that's all."

"Sometimes getting busy is all it takes. And then, before you know it, you're part of the town."

"You're wrong," Syd told him. "I'm still a New Yorker."

"Well okay, if you say so. But what's keeping you so busy?"

"You are."

"Me?"

"Well, I'm not sure, but I think it's you."

"What about me?"

"Well," Syd began slowly, sorting things out as she went along, "I met a man whose name is Joseph Stowe. And he makes dolls that look like people who lived here when you did."

"What kind of dolls?"

"Let's see. There are four of them, and they look just like real people. There's an old-man doll, who's painting a toy watch. He has white hair, but you can't see his face. Then there's another man, who's blond and kind of fat, and he has a basket of bread on his arm."

"A basket of bread?" Jake said. His voice sounded surprised.

"Uh-huh."

"And the other two?"

"There's a little girl in a funny red suit, and she has a bag of marbles in her hand."

"What does she look like?"

"Let's see," Syd said. "She has dark hair and very light skin, and . . ."

"And?"

"Well, she's really sad."

"And the last one?" Jaked asked.

"I think he's a basketball player. His arm's in the air like he's reaching for something."

Jake didn't say anything.

"Jake?" Syd said.

"I'm here. Why do you think they look like people who lived in the town when I did?"

"Because I saw a book that was published in 1900, and their pictures were in it."

"You know—" Jake began. But then he stopped.

"Jake?" Syd said again.

"Those dolls sound a lot like my family. My grandfather was a toy maker. And my father was a baker."

"Did you have a sister?"

"Yes," Jake said, so softly that Syd could barely hear him. "And she loved to play marbles."

"Was she sad?"

"Not while I was there. I remember her laughing all the time."

All of a sudden Syd remembered something. "What was your father's name?"

"Peter. Why?"

"Because I . . ."

Syd had started to tell Jake about the newspaper articles. But something made her stop. "Do you want to talk to mom?" she asked instead.

"I'd love to."

"The dolls are his family," Syd told her father when she came out of the study.

"Did you mention what you read in the paper—about Parkersburg thinking he'd been murdered?"

Syd shook her head.

"Why not?"

"I almost did. But I think—well, if I'd told him, then he'd know that the town had been mean to his family after he'd left, and he might think it was his fault. And then he'd be really sad."

Mr. Stowe looked at his daughter and smiled. "You know," he said, "sometimes you make me proud to be your father."

Syd smiled angelically and drew an imaginary halo above her head with her finger.

Mr. Stowe laughed and went into the study. Syd heard him ask her mother for the phone.

In a little while he came out. "He wants to say good-bye."

Syd picked up the receiver. "Hi, Jake," she said.

"I just wanted to ask you about this man who made the dolls."

"Well, he's an old man, and his granddaughter is my friend. Remember, the girl named Laura?"

"I wonder how he knows about my family."

"Maybe he's a relative."

"I guess he could be," Jake said thoughtfully. "My grandfather had some brothers, so I guess there could be some more Stowes wandering around."

"Well, I'm going to try and find him, and I'll tell you what I find out."

"You do that," said Jake.

"Say hello to Jill when you see her. And tell her I'll write."

Syd hung up the phone. Then she sat down at her mother's desk and put a piece of paper into the typewriter. Maybe if she wrote it down it would make sense.

1. The dolls are supposed to be Jake's family.
2. The family who lived on Lake Drive in 1901 was also Jake's family.
3. Therefore—the doll family and the 1901 Stowe family are the same.
4. Who is Mr. Stowe the doll maker? And who is Laura?

Syd's father came into the study. "Busy?"

"No."

"Jake wanted me to tell you something."

"What?"

"Well, we talked about the basketball player. He said he never played basketball. But since all the other dolls match his family, that one must be him."

"If the doll's not playing basketball, what's he doing?"

"Well, you know how Jake always dreamed of leaving Parkersburg? He thinks the doll is reaching for that dream."

14

"There it is," Syd said, as she helped her parents spread out the blanket. "I don't think it looks haunted. It just looks like an old house to me."

It was a perfect day for swimming. The sun was shining brightly, and there were no clouds in sight. "This was a great idea," Mr. Stowe said. "I'm glad I thought of it."

"*You* didn't think of it!" Syd cried. "*I* did!"

Mr. Stowe laughed. He was always saying things like that. And Syd always reacted the same way.

They studied the house for a few minutes. "If you really want to know," Mrs. Stowe said at last, "I think it looks like a lovely old house. As a matter of fact, I'd like to get my hands on it. I'll bet I could make it into something."

Syd flopped down on the blanket and turned onto her stomach. "Well," she asked, "are you ready to meet your relatives?"

Mrs. Stowe stretched and turned over onto her back. "Tell

you what," she sighed. "Give me just one hour of this wonderful sun, and then we'll tackle Mr. Stowe and his haunted house."

Syd moaned and said, "An *hour!* Bro-ther!"

Her parents laughed and closed their eyes.

Syd sat up and looked at the house. She couldn't tell much about it from this distance, except that it was old and needed paint. It also looked as if no one lived there. Haunted! she thought. Houses aren't really haunted!

She stood up and brushed the sand from her legs. "I'm going for a walk."

"Shhh," her father whispered. "Your mother's asleep. Just be careful."

Syd had been walking next to the water for about ten minutes when she decided to explore the house. She made her way around the sunbathers, and ran across the sand to the trees that separated the beach from the road. When she reached the trees, she stopped and looked up at the house. Then she crossed the road and began to climb. The hill was rocky, and much steeper than it had looked from the beach.

Halfway up, she sat on a rock to rest. She could see the beach from where she sat, and it was easy to pick out her parents' red blanket. She could see the people, but she couldn't hear them. And she could see the water, but she couldn't hear it either. "It's weird," she whispered. For a minute, she thought of going back. But then she changed her mind. I've started this, she thought, and I'm going to finish it.

At the top of the hill, she leaned against a tree to catch her breath. The house stood before her, looking bigger and shabbier than it had from below. *Shabby*'s a nice word for it, she thought. Not only was it badly in need of paint, it also needed a new roof, a new porch, and maybe even a new third floor. Boards were nailed over the windows in the front of the house.

Syd made her way through the overgrown grass and pulled at the boards. But they were nailed securely, and she could not loosen them. She moved around the house, inspecting the windows, and trying to find a way to see inside. But it was no use. Every window was boarded tightly shut.

She climbed up onto the long front porch and knocked on the door. Wouldn't it be something, she thought, if Laura appeared and invited me in for lunch. But no one answered. She turned the handle on the front door slowly, while scenes from old horror movies flashed through her mind. But it was locked. She put her ear next to the door and listened.

If this house is haunted, she thought, I'll hear something. A moan, a creak, or something. But the house was silent.

Syd jumped off the porch and walked slowly away from the house. Nobody lives in *that* place, she thought, as she climbed down the hill. Nobody's lived there in a long, long time. Either there's another Lake Drive in this town, or the librarian misunderstood Mr. Stowe.

Syd's parents were asleep when she reached the blanket. She sat down and ran her hands through the sand. Then she dug her feet in deep, and began to bury her legs. A baby was crying somewhere down the beach, and Syd looked up to see where the noise was coming from. The baby was lying next to its mother on a blanket. Beyond the baby, far down the beach, an old man and a girl were walking in the water. As they came closer, Syd saw that it was Mr. Stowe and Laura. Just then, Mr. Stowe looked up and saw her. He took Laura's hand, turned, and walked quickly away.

15

Syd jumped up and ran down the beach. Glancing over his shoulder, Mr. Stowe ran too, pulling Laura behind him. They crossed the sand and disappeared into the trees. Syd followed, but when she reached the trees, they were nowhere in sight.

She stopped and looked up and down the empty road. Then she searched the hill in front of her. They were running up the hill, heading for the house at the top. She stood behind a tree and watched, wanting to follow, but not sure if she should. Why was Mr. Stowe trying to avoid her? Why didn't he want her around?

I ought to go back to the blanket and go to sleep, Syd thought. I ought to forget this whole thing.

But there were so many things that she wanted to ask Laura. Why hadn't Laura told her that her grandfather was Mr. Stowe? And why hadn't she just come right out and said, "My grandfather made the dolls"? But most of all she wanted to find out if they were really friends.

Syd looked back up the hill, but Mr. Stowe and Laura had disappeared.

"They're in that house," she said out loud. "I don't know how they got in, but I know they're in there."

She waited for a minute, and then she began to run, without stopping, straight up the hill. The house stood before her, silent, dark, and unchanged. The windows were still covered with boards. The front door was tightly closed. And there was no sign that anyone had entered anywhere.

Syd tiptoed across the yard and listened at one of the boarded windows. Nothing. She made her way from window to window, trying to find a way that Mr. Stowe and Laura might have gotten in.

Moving in slow motion, she crept up the steps to the small back porch and turned the doorknob.

The door sprang silently open.

She leaned against the back of the house to catch her breath and wait until her heart was quiet again. Then she tiptoed through the doorway and stood in the dark hall.

A soft light was shining through the open doorway across the hall. Syd moved toward it, stopped, breathed deeply, then leaned around and looked in.

The light was coming from two large candles that were sitting on a heavy dark table at the far end of the room. Syd stood by the door and studied the faces of the three people who sat in the shadows around the table. She recognized Laura first. Her small arms were resting on one end of the table, and she seemed lost in the tall chair in which she was sitting.

Syd started to speak, but when she saw the blond man sitting beside Laura, her stomach jumped, and she stopped. She took a deep breath and let it out slowly, as she tried to make some sense out of what she was seeing. Seated beside Laura, his bread basket on the table in front of him, was Peter Stowe, looking just as he had in the library book, the one that had been published in 1900.

At the other end of the table, facing Laura, an old man sat silent and unmoving. His back was to Syd, and she could not see his face. His white hair hung over the collar of his shirt, and from the back he looked just like the old-man doll.

Syd closed her eyes, unable to believe what they were telling her. But when she opened them, the scene hadn't changed. They were all there: Laura, the bread man, and the toy maker, looking just as they had seventy-eight years ago.

Syd stood by the door, letting it all sink in, until her legs began to tire and she had to lean back. As she touched the door, it flew back and hit the wall with a crash.

She grabbed the doorknob to regain her balance. Then she turned and looked at the table. Laura and the bread man were staring at her. But the old man had not moved. His back was still to Syd.

"Excuse me," she said, moving backward through the door. "I . . ." She hesitated, then changed her mind and began to walk across the room toward the table. The looks on Laura's and Peter Stowe's faces changed from surprise to alarm as they watched her.

She stopped at the old man's chair and looked down at his face. It was Joseph Stowe, the doll maker. Mr. Stowe, she now understood, had made a doll of himself.

Syd put her hand on Joseph Stowe's chair and looked at Laura. Laura was smiling at her.

"Who are you?" Syd whispered.

72

"I'm sorry," Laura said softly. "I wanted to tell you so many times."

"Tell me what?"

But Laura bent her head, private once again.

"There are some things it is better not to explain," Joseph Stowe said. Then he too turned away.

Syd didn't know what else to say or do, so she lowered her hand and walked slowly from the room.

When she reached the blanket, her parents were awake.

"Are you ready to tackle Mr. Stowe?" her mother asked.

"I just went up there, and there's nobody home."

"You went up there all alone?" her father asked. He sounded very impressed.

"Of course."

"Well, what's it like?"

"It's really old and, well, I doubt if anyone has lived there for a long, long time."

"The librarian must have given you the wrong address," her mother said. "But Mr. Stowe will show up, you'll see, and then you can find out if they're relatives." She turned over onto her stomach and closed her eyes.

It's not really a lie, Syd thought. Anyway, what can I say? There are three people sitting in that weird house up there, and they all look just like people who lived in 1900? They wouldn't believe that. And maybe I shouldn't believe it either. Maybe this whole thing is a wild, crazy dream.

Syd buried her feet in the sand and wondered if she would ever see Laura again.

16

"Do you think it will ever stop raining?" Syd asked her mother on Monday morning. "It rained all day yesterday, and now it's raining again. I'm going stir crazy."

"It'll stop," Mrs. Stowe told her. "It always does. Why don't you read a book today? It'll get your mind off that house."

Syd still hadn't told her mother about what she had seen in the house. She was afraid to tell anyone. Who would believe her? She still wasn't sure she believed it herself.

Syd went up to her room, took a book from the shelf, and lay down on her bed. She read the first sentence six times before she closed the book and went to the window. The rain was stopping, and she could see the sun through the clouds.

"I'm going for a bike ride," she told her mother.

Mrs. Stowe looked out of the window. "Try to get back early."

Syd knew just where she was going—to find Laura and try to get some answers.

74

When she reached Lake Drive, she leaned her bike against a tree and ran up the hill without stopping. She went straight to the back of the house, climbed the porch steps, and turned the knob. The house was quiet.

She took a moment to swallow the lump of fear that had lodged in her throat. Then she walked across the hall and opened the door.

The room was dark. The candles were gone, and the only light came from a small crack in one of the boarded windows. She ran her hand along the wall, searching for a light switch. But there wasn't one. She followed the twig of light with her eyes. Someone had placed an old grayed sheet over the table and chairs where the Stowes had been sitting. There was no one in the room.

Syd walked across the room and lifted a corner of the sheet. Then she sat in the uncovered chair and looked around her. The two candles that had been on the table two days before were on a counter near her chair, and she picked up one of them. She lighted it with a match that she found on the counter. Then, carrying it high to light her way, she began to explore.

The room seemed to be a large kitchen with a metal stove in the center. Jake had told Syd about stoves like this one, wood-burning stoves that people had cooked on when he was a boy.

Still carrying the candle, Syd tiptoed over to an old wooden box with two compartments, which stood beside the sink. It was almost as tall as she was. She opened the top compartment, remembering that Jake had said something about refrigerators that were made of wood. You put large blocks of ice in the top part of the refrigerator, and that's how the food in the bottom part stayed cold.

Syd went back to the table and replaced the corner of the sheet. Then she closed the door softly behind her and moved down the hall.

Sheets that had once been white covered most of the furniture in the small parlor and the living room. One of the few pieces that wasn't covered was a large dark piano that stood against one wall of the parlor. Syd sat down on the small round stool and played "Chopsticks," the one song she knew. When she was finished, she noticed a small window in the piano in which there was a roll of music, and she thought, This is one of those old player pianos that plays by itself. But when she pumped the pedals with her feet, nothing happened. After trying for five minutes to fix it, she gave up and walked across the room to a bookcase with a glass front. She opened it carefully and, holding the candle close to the books inside, tried to make out the titles. The books on the top shelf seemed to be adult books, with titles like *Ben Hur* and *Quo Vadis*. But the other shelves held many of the same books that Syd had in her bedroom at home: books like *Black Beauty, The Adventures of Huckleberry Finn,* and *Little Men* and *Little Women*.

Syd returned to the kitchen, blew out the candle, and put it back on the counter. Then she went outside, walked around to the front of the house, and sat on an old swing that was hanging in a corner of the porch. She stayed there for a long time, swinging gently, while she tried to decide what to do.

17

After a while, she stood up and walked around the grounds. In a far corner of the backyard she saw something that she hadn't seen before, and she moved closer to get a better look. It was a small cemetery which contained several tiny gravestones.

There were three stones, very close together, near her feet, and she knelt down on one knee to read the words which were carved into them.

LAURA STOWE	PETER STOWE	JOSEPH STOWE
BORN 1892	BORN 1862	BORN 1841
DIED JULY 25, 1903	DIED JULY 25, 1903	DIED JULY 25, 1903

She stood up and walked through the cemetery, reading the words on the other stones carefully. She did not recognize any of the first names, but they were all Stowes. As she was about to leave, she noticed one last gravestone and she knelt down to read it.

"Laura's mother," Syd whispered.

Syd walked back to the house and sat on the bottom step. A chill passed over her and she shivered. All three of them died together, she thought.

She rubbed her arms to warm them. On the beach below, a lone swimmer was standing at the edge of the water. Syd watched as he raised his arms, hesitated, then lowered them and walked back to his towel.

They're ghosts, Syd thought. They're really ghosts.

The swimmer stood and studied the cold water.

"Laura too," Syd whispered. "No wonder they didn't want to talk to me. They didn't want me to know."

The swimmer took a step, hesitated, then raced across the sand and plunged in.

They took the book and the doll because I was getting too close, Syd thought. But why did they wait all these years to come back?

In less than a minute, the swimmer emerged from the water and ran back to the warmth of his towel.

They came back because of me, Syd thought. They came back because they heard that someone named Stowe had moved here, and they thought we might be able to clear their name.

Syd climbed slowly down the hill. When she reached the bottom, she stopped and looked up at the big white house.

As she rode back to town, she remembered the tiny toy watch, and she understood why the hands were pointing to the twelve. Time must have stopped for these people at midnight on the night that Jake went away, she thought. And maybe now it can start again.

Syd parked her bike in front of the library and went inside. The man who had helped her with the microfilm machine was standing behind the desk, and he waved as she passed.

She went over to the drawer where the microfilm was stored and took out the film of the *Parkersburg Times* for the week of July 25, 1903. Then she threaded it into the machine and sat down to read. When she was finished, she put the film away and went over to the desk.

"What's up?" the librarian asked.

"I'm still reading about that family up on Lake Drive."

"Anything new?"

"Well," Syd said, "I just read their obituary, and it looks like they all died at the same time, in a boating accident. It was a couple of years after that murder thing."

The man looked down at Syd thoughtfully. "You know," he said, "I think you've really stumbled onto a story."

"I know."

"It would make an awfully good story for the *Kid's Gazette*."

"I was thinking the same thing," said Syd. "But it's really more interesting than you think, because nobody killed anybody, and I can prove it."

Syd was referring to Jake. The ghosts of Lake Drive would have to remain her secret.

"How?" the man asked.

Syd drummed her fingers on the desk. "I think I'll let you wait until I write it up for the paper."

"Say," the librarian said, "do you remember that book you were looking for?"

"This Is Parkersburg?"

"That's the one. Well, that old man returned it."

"Did he say anything?"

"I asked him how he could live in the house on Lake Drive, and he said he'd lived there for a long time, but that now he was going to move on."

"Did you ask him what he meant?"

"Yes, and he said that his work here was finished, and that now he was free."

18

Syd woke up at eight thirty the next morning. She jumped out of bed and opened the curtains. It was a bright summer day, the kind of day that calls for special things. She went over to her desk, took out some stationery, and sat down to write to Jake.

She had stayed awake for a long time the night before, trying to think of a way to answer the questions that she was sure were bothering him. She knew that he was wondering who Joseph Stowe was, and how he knew enough about his family to make the dolls. But Syd also knew that she couldn't tell him that Mr. Stowe was a ghost. At about midnight she had decided what to do. She had decided to tell a little white lie.

Dear Jake,

This is just a short letter to tell you that I found out who the doll maker is. He's just a man who lives in a town near here, and he makes dolls. He isn't a relative or anything like that, even though his name is Stowe.

And he did use that book to make the dolls.

Love,
Syd

I can't tell him any more, she thought. Because no matter what I say, he'll figure it all out. And then he'll know how his family suffered after he left.

When she put down her pen, it was nine o'clock and the phone was ringing.

"It's for you," her mother called from downstairs.

Syd went into her parents' room and picked up the extension. She heard a click as her mother hung up the downstairs phone.

"Syd?" a woman's voice said.

"This is Syd."

"It's Mrs. Diaz."

"Oh hi."

"Can you come down to the store today? I've got something for you."

"Sure," Syd said. "What is it?"

"Let's save it till you get here, okay?"

"Okay. I'll be right down."

She hung up the phone and ran into her room. It took her less than ten minutes to dress and comb her hair. As she was running through the kitchen, she remembered the letter and she ran back upstairs, put a stamp on it, and stuffed it into the back pocket of her jeans.

"No breakfast?" her mother asked when she came back downstairs.

"I'll be back."

Syd jumped on her bike and rode down the sidewalk. When

84

she passed the jump rope players, she must have been going twenty. One of the girls shouted "Hey!" and she screeched to a stop and circled back. It was the girl who had wanted to learn some skateboard tricks.

"Hey!" she said. "Are you going to show me those tricks?"

"Sure. How about this afternoon?"

"Great!"

Syd put her foot on the pedal. But then she thought of something, and she walked her bike closer to the girl.

"How about this?" she said. "You teach me to play jump rope and well, uh, kickball. . . ."

"You don't know how to play *kickball*?"

"I guess I never learned. But if you'll teach me, I'll teach you my skateboard tricks."

The girl smiled, held out her hand, and said, "It's a deal."

Syd shook the girl's hand. "One o'clock?" she called, as she rode down the street.

"One o'clock!"

19

Mrs. Diaz was waiting on a customer when Syd arrived. "I'll be right with you," she said. "I've got news."

Syd leaned against the counter and waited.

"What is it?" she asked, when the customer was gone.

"Guess who came in last night?"

"Mr. Stowe?" Syd cried.

"That's right. He brought back the sad-eyed doll. But she isn't very sad any more."

Mrs. Diaz reached under the counter and took out a box. "Open it," she said.

Syd opened the box and took out the doll that was inside. The funny red suit was the same. The haircut was the same. And the tiny suede bag was the same. There was only one thing different. "The face," she whispered. "Did you see the face?"

"I saw it."

"It's beautiful," Syd said softly.

She picked up the doll and looked at Laura's face. There were

tiny lines around the eyes, tiny little laugh lines. She ran her finger across the lips. It was a small change, but what a difference it made.

"She's smiling."

"I guess we can't call her sad-eyed girl anymore."

Syd smoothed the doll's dress and hair. A small piece of paper was sticking out of the suede bag, and she pulled it out and unrolled it. She found the magnifying glass and read:

> Dear Syd,
>
> I'm sorry we won't get to work on that newspaper together. You'll be a great reporter. I know you will.
>
> > Your good friend,
> > Laura

Tears came to Syd's eyes. She rolled up the paper and put it back into the little bag. Mrs. Diaz was looking at her and smiling. "Mr. Stowe said that he'd like you to have all four of the dolls."

Syd studied the dolls. The basketball player wasn't reaching anymore. Someone had moved his arm so that it rested at his side. And whoever had done it had also moved him very close to the bread man and placed the bread man's left hand on his son's shoulder.

"I can't take them," Syd said. "You can sell them for a lot of money."

Mrs. Diaz took out a large box and put it on the counter. Then, one by one, she took down the dolls and packed them. "They never really belonged to me," she said. "They belonged to Mr. Stowe. And now they belong to you." She handed the box to Syd. "They're yours. Enjoy them."

"Oh, I will."

Syd left her bike at the toy store and walked downtown. When she got to the drugstore, she went inside and sat in the last booth. She put the box on the table in front of her and ordered a cup of hot chocolate. Then she took the letter to Jake out of her pocket and reread it. She was trying to think of a way to tell him that his family had come to understand, or at least accept, him. But every time she thought of a way, she realized that it would either raise questions in Jake's mind or make him feel sad about his family. So she put the letter back into her pocket, unchanged.

When the waitress brought the hot chocolate, Syd thanked her and leaned against the wall. She stretched her legs out on the seat in front of her and settled back to study the people. If a new girl had glanced in the window at just that moment, she would have thought that Sydell Stowe had been living in Parkersburg forever.